Buzz bum, buzz bum

Buzz bum, buzz, bum bum bum

How Butterbees™ Came to Bee!

by **Lana Grimm & Tania Bloch**   *Illustrated by* **David Michener**
with additional verse by **Donna Michener**

Special acknowledgements to:

Roy E. Grimm and Solomon and Joyce
Bloch, for their patience, love and support.
Karen Grencik, David and Donna Michener,
for believing in our vision. Lana's children,
Adi and Shalev, for being our teachers.
Joe and Maleita Wise, for their creative
consulting and encouragement. Larry
Lindahl, for his design expertise and
patience.

Published by Bee Unlimited Inc.
P.O. Box 20364, Sedona AZ 86341
888-321-1717
www.beeunlimited.com

SECOND EDITION

Illustrated by
David Michener

Additional Verse by
Donna Michener

Edited by
Karen Grencik

Book Design by
Larry Lindahl

Printed by
Worzalla Publishing
in the United States of America

Publisher's Cataloging-in-Publication

Grimm, Lana.
    How butterbees came to bee! / by Lana
Grimm and Tania Bloch ; with additional
verse by Donna Michener ; illustrated by
David Michener. --Sedona, AZ : Bee
Unlimited, 2001.

    p. cm.

ISBN 0966204832
    1. Bees--Poetry. 2. Stories in rhyme.
I. Bloch, Tania. II. Michener, Donna. III.
Michener, David. IV. Title.

PZ7.G756 How 2001   2001-89094
[E]--dc21 CIP

Dedicated to
all the children of the world

Bee Calm

One magical, calm, spring day,
In red rock canyons far away,
Bright **butterflies** and buzzing **bees**,
Greeted cacti, flowers, and trees.

Buzz hum, buzz hum, buzz, hum hum hum

On this bright and sunny day,
A **bee** went out to work and play.
Buzzing happily in the sun,
Flower to flower, having fun.

Buzz hum, buzz hum, buzz, hum hum hum

A handsome **butterfly** floated by,
Curious to see what's up, and why.
"Little Miss Bee, what is your name?
What are you doing, playing a game?"

7

"My friends call me **Bonnie Bee**.
I'm as busy as I can be.
I carry pollen to and fro.
This helps the **baby flowers** grow.

Buzz hum, buzz hum, buzz, hum hum hum

I collect nectar for the hive,
Making **honey** to stay alive.
We keep our beehive neat and clean,
And work together for our **Queen**."

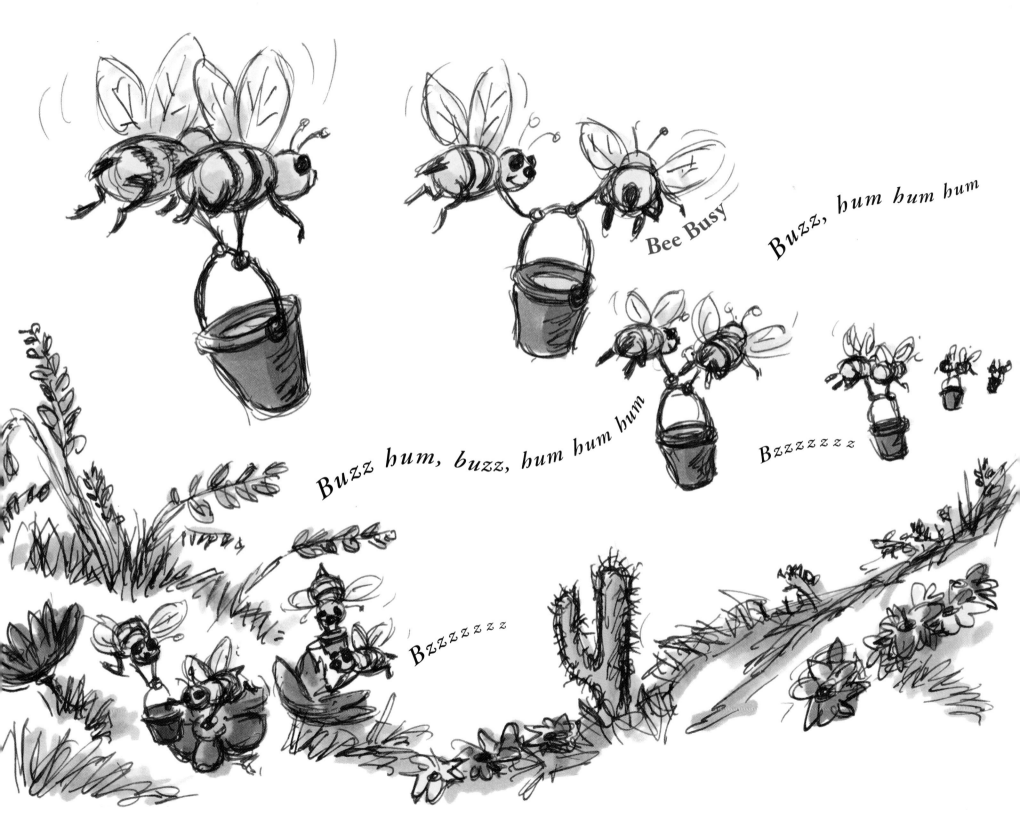

Bee Busy

Buzz, hum hum hum

Buzz hum, buzz, hum hum hum

Bzzzzzzz

Bzzzzzzz

"Enough about me,
  how about you?
What's your **name**,
  and what do you do?"

10

"They call me
Benny Butterfly.
I'm really sort of
humble and shy."

"I'm a **caterpillar** at the start,
But we butterflies are very smart.

Bee Smart

A silken **cocoon** we learn to spin,
To keep us safe and warm within.

While inside, we gently change form,
So that new butterflies can be born."

Bee Safe

13

"When I awake from this **deep sleep**,
From my cocoon I slowly creep.

I spread my **wings** out
as they dry,
And begin my life
as a **butterfly.**

Bonnie, you may not
believe all this,
It's called a
met-a-mor-pho-sis!"

Bee Alive

They **played** as friends, dancing in the sun,
Sharing stories, games, and having fun.
From that day on, they met each day,
Becoming **best friends** in every way.

Buzz hum, buzz hum, buzz, hum hum hum

But one spring day they played past five,
Way past the **curfew** of the hive.
"Oh, Benny, I'm worried about my Queen,
When she's mad, she's really **mean!**"

Buzz hum, buzz hum, buzz, hum hum hum

Quickly, Bonnie made a beeline home,
Hoping her queen had left her throne.
Perhaps she could slip into the hive,

But . . .

Buzz hum, buzz hum, buzz, hum hum

Bee Prompt

19

. . . Guard Bees waited,
            not one but *five*!

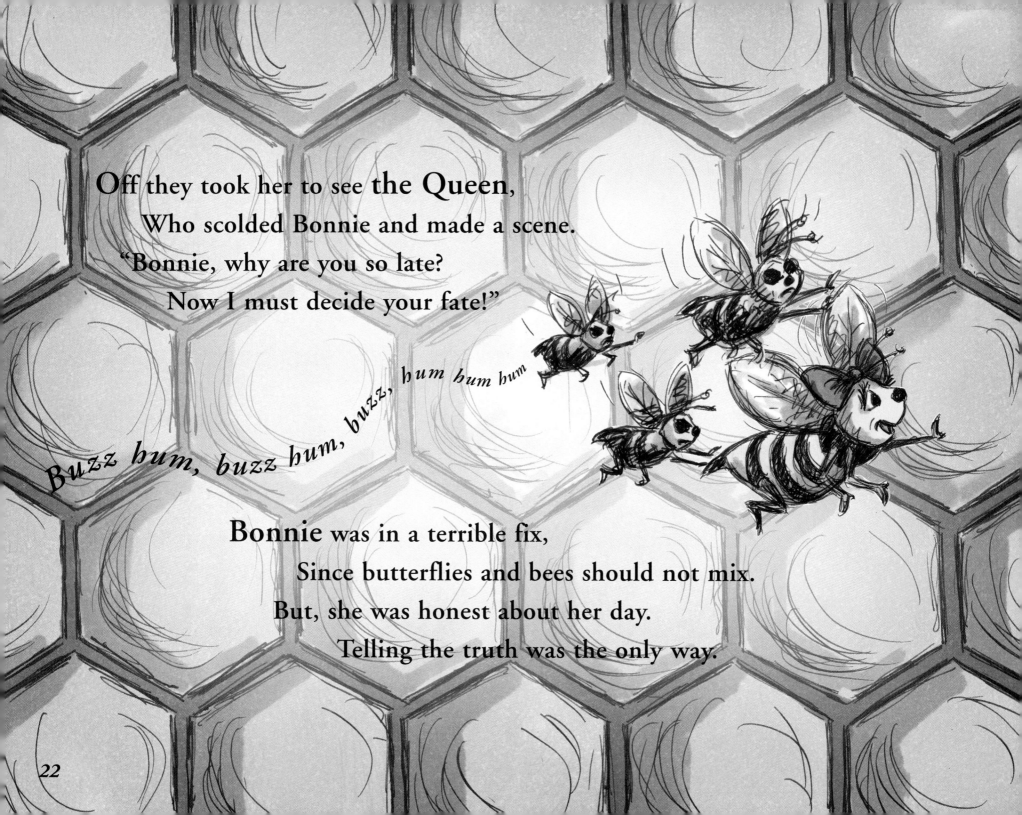

Off they took her to see the Queen,
Who scolded Bonnie and made a scene.
"Bonnie, why are you so late?
Now I must decide your fate!"

Buzz hum, buzz hum, buzz, hum hum hum

Bonnie was in a terrible fix,
Since butterflies and bees should not mix.
But, she was honest about her day.
Telling the truth was the only way.

"Although I am proud you did not lie,
You must be punished and you know why.

You are now grounded, back in the hive,
To **sweep**, **clean** and **dust**, from five to five!

You'll sleep in the drone cells alone at night.
Guard Bees! Take her from my sight!"

Bzzzzzz

24

Meanwhile . . .

. . .Worried and sad,
Benny flew to the creek,
Waiting . . . day by day,
week by week.

Benny asked his friends,
"What should I do?"
Rolf Rattlesnake hissed,
"I haven't a clue!"

But Uqualla Quail,
known to be wise,
Noticed the sadness
in Benny's eyes.

"Be patient," she said,
   "follow your heart.
Listen inside
   to your knowing part."

Buzz hum, buzz, hum hum hum

Bee Free

28

Then it came, the sweetest song,
  One he'd not heard, for, oh, so long.
"Could it be my Bonnie Bee,
  Is once again, buzzing free!"

Buzz hum, buzz hum, buzz, hum hum hum

"Oh, Bonnie, how I've missed you so,
  Seeing you sets my heart aglow."
"Oh, Benny, I have missed you too,
  Afraid I'd never again find you."

They flew to their place by the creek,
Taking the time to share and speak.
Benny suggested with a smile,
"Let's just sit and be still awhile."

Benny listened to his knowing part,
And heard the words, *"Follow your heart."*
He whispered, "Bonnie, will you be mine?"
"Oh, yes," she sighed, "till the end of time."

Buzz hum, buzz hum, buzz, hum hum hum

Bee Caring

All creatures and rocks smiled to see,
These two wed in **love's harmony**.
Uqualla Quail, standing proud and tall,
Sounded her love song marriage call.

Bee Loving

33

Then one day to their utmost joy . . .

Bee Joyful

. . . Butterbees were born, a **girl** and **boy!**
They named them Bizzy and Buzzy,
Both so cute, cuddly, and fuzzy.
With **bee bodies** and **butterfly wings**,
Babee butterbees are amazing things!

Buzz hum, buzz hum, buzz, hum hum hum

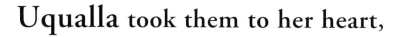

Uqualla took them to her heart,
Wanting the babees to have the best start.
She took them under her loving wing,
Telling wise tales that life can bring.

36

She said . . .
"Inside there is a knowing place,
Where lives the soul
and loving grace.

It helps us when
we're feeling sad,
To know these feelings
aren't so bad.

It helps us see
others as they are,
Accepting all creatures,
near and far."

Bee Accepting

The **Queen** got word
　　of what **Uqualla** said.
Thoughts went 'round and 'round
　　in her head.

One day she awoke,
　　as from a dream,
　　The Queen felt happy,
　　not quite so mean.

She'd always loved
　　Bonnie in her heart,
And felt it was time
　　to make a new start.

The Queen had
a happy and smiling face,
Now that she'd found
her own **knowing place**.

Hearing the news
of the Butterbees' birth,
She began to dance
with glee and mirth.

So . . .

That's the tale of how we came to bee,
    Bizzy and Buzzy Butterbee.
    We float like butterflies, buzz like bees,
        Pollinate flowers, cacti, and trees.

Buzz hum, buzz hum, buzz, hum hum hum

We gather pollen in pollen sacs,
    And fix our home with strong beeswax.
We spin silk, make honey, and sweet bee bread,
    And collect nectar till time for bed.

We bet you're blessed with talents, too.
    Why don't *you* try to name a few?"

Bee
Creative

Bee Kind

"*Hive 'n Seek* is our favorite game,
Finding 'Bee ways' that we can name.
Bee helpful and wise, bee loving and true.
Bee happy, bee kind, and just bee you!"

Buzz hum, buzz hum, buzz, hum hum hum

As the golden sun sets in the west,
It's once again **time for all to rest.**

Bizzy and Buzzy lay down to sleep,
Hugging each other with love so deep.
Drifting in night's sweet wonderlands,
Humming this prayer and holding hands . . .
"Whatever happens to you and me,
Help us to bee the **best we can bee.**"

Buzz hum, buzz hum, buzz, hum hum hum

Shhh . . . Bee still . . .
you may hear the hum.

Just Bee You!

Buzz hum, buzz hum, buzz, hum hum hum

**Bonnie
Bee**

**Benny
Butterfly**

Buzz hum, buzz, hum, buzz, hum hum hum

Queen

**Rolf
Rattlesnake**

46

Bizzy Butterbee

Buzzy Butterbee

Buzz hum, buzz hum, buzz, hum hum hum

Bye, bye from us all,
And let's bee **friends!**

Rumpledink Rabbit

Uqualla Quail

47

About the Authors

LANA GRIMM and TANIA BLOCH are sisters and colleagues whose working lives have centered around helping others. Both are Certified Yoga Teachers, artists, and the founders of Bee Unlimited. Tania has a Master's in Psychology and Lana has practiced as a Registered Nurse.

Lana and Tania's fun-loving Butterbee plush toys and picture books were born from their love of Sedona, bees, butterflies, and children. Their vision for the Butterbees is that they help empower children to tap into their own unique talents, encourage them to value one another's differences, and to help develop their self-esteem. Tania cherishes a beloved friendship that was the seed of inspiration for the Butterbee story.

Both sisters have overcome tremendous challenges in their personal lives. They hope to inspire the belief that, like the amazing bee and butterfly, "Anything is possible!"

About the Illustrator

DAVID MICHENER was a key artist for Walt Disney Studios until his retirement in 1987. He then returned to teaching at California Institute of the Arts in Valencia, hoping to inspire future artists with his love of animation and film and to give something back to the industry he had contributed to for so many years.

He has since directed several animated films for Hanna Barbera and is often asked to lecture to the young animators of today.

He and his wife Donna have been married for nearly fifty years, have three daughters and six grandchildren, all of whom are very proud of his many talents.